panda series

PANDA books are for first readers beginning to make their own way through books.

Spotty Sally

Anne Marie Herron
• Pictures by Stephen Hall •

THE O'BRIEN PRESS
DUBLIN

First published 2000 by The O'Brien Press Ltd,
12 Terenure Road East, Rathgar, Dublin 6, Ireland.
Tel: +353 1 4923333; Fax: +353 1 4922777
E-mail: books@obrien.ie
Website: www.obrien.ie
Reprinted 2002, 2004, 2006.

ISBN-10: 0-86278-640-1
ISBN-13: 978-0-86278-640-3

British Library Cataloguing-in-Publication Data
Herron, Anne Marie
Spotty Sally. - (O'Brien pandas ; 16)
1.Children's stories
I.Title II.Hall, Stephen
823.9'14[J]

4   5   6   7   8   9   10
06   07   08   09   10

The O'Brien Press receives
assistance from

the arts
council
chomhairle
ealaíon

layout, editing, design: The O'Brien Press Ltd
Printing: Cox & Wyman Ltd

Can YOU spot the panda
hidden in the story?

It all began when Sally
was a tiny baby.

She had dark curly hair,
a turned up nose,
a yawny little smile
and a **rosy pink spot**
on each of her dimpled cheeks.

Sally's Mum wrapped Sally up
in a cosy spotted blanket.

'What a lovely little
spotted baby,'
said Sally's Mum.

'Spots suit her,'
said Sally's Grandma.

And that was how it all began.

Soon afterwards Sally got
a spotty hat,
a spotty jumper,
spotty dungarees
and spotty bootees
with little spotty ribbons.

She even got spotty pyjamas
and a spotty dressing gown.

When Sally was **one**
she had a cake with
spots on top
and a spotty ribbon
going all around.

I AM A BIG 1

Sally blew out her
one little spotty candle.
She smiled and her
two little spotty cheeks glowed.

'Spots,' said Sally
in her little baby voice.

When Sally was **two**
she got more spotty presents.
She got a spotty scarf
from her Grandma,
a spotty tea-set from Grandad,
a spotty bag from Aunt Jane
and a spotty dinosaur
from her Mum and Dad.

Everyone cheered as
Sally blew out her
two spotty candles and said,
'I like spots.'

And Sally really did like spots.

She liked to look at
spotty ladybirds in the garden.
She liked to draw spots
on her copybooks.

And once when she was ill
she looked in the mirror
for hours and hours
smiling at her **spotty face**.
She was sorry when the spots
went away.

When Sally was **three**
she got a great surprise.
When she had blown out
her three spotty
birthday candles
Mum and Dad gave her
a special present.

It was a cute little dog
for Sally to play with.
Sally squealed with delight
when she saw him.

'I know just what I will call him,' she said.

And, yes, I'm sure you've guessed. She called him –

When Sally was **four**
she got even more
spotty presents.
She got a spotty football
from Grandma,

a spotty money-box
from Grandad,

a spotty bed cover
from Aunt Jane,

a spotty lamp
from Dad,

and a spotty bear, dressed as a
pilot, that Mum had brought
home on her aeroplane.
(Sally's Mum was a pilot.)

Sally blew out her four
spotty candles and said,
'**More spots** for Sally.'

I am Four

Everyone smiled.

'Sally really **loves spots**,'

they all said.

But the truth was that
Sally was getting
tired of spots.
When she looked around her,
all she could see was **spots**.

26

There were spots on the walls
and spots on the bed,
spots on the toy box
and spots on the floor,
spots on the chair
and spots on the ceiling.

There were spots
everywhere.

And everything she owned
had spots.
Her books had spots.
Her dolls had spots.
Her clothes and shoes
and toys had spots.
Her new schoolbag had spots.

a spotty story

Even Sally's knickers
had spots.

The trouble was that
everyone thought Sally
still loved spots.
At Christmas she got
spotty decorations for the tree.

At Easter she got eggs
with spots on them.
When people went on holidays
they sent her postcards
with spots.

A view of the Hotel.

And they brought back
spotty t-shirts that said
silly things like:
**Spotted you
on holidays**.

Spotted you on Holidays

Tee Hee

Yes, Sally was getting
very, very tired of spots.
In fact, the spots were
driving her crazy.

'Spots, spots and more spots,
she screamed.
**'I'm sick and tired
of spots**.'

Sally decided to do something
about it. She would tell
everyone that she
did not like spots.

And she would tell them now
before she was five.

She did not want another
spotty birthday.

Yes, she would tell them
right away.

35

First, she tried to tell Grandma.

'Grandma,' said Sally,
'you know how I always
get spotty things
for my birthday? Well –'

'I do indeed,' said Grandma,
'and don't you worry,
I've already got a
super spotty present for you.'

'Oh,' said Sally.

Then she tried to tell Grandad.

'Grandad,' she said,
'about the spots –'

I know,' said Grandad.
'I've got a lovely spotty surprise
for your birthday.'

'Oh,' said Sally.

And then she tried to tell
Aunt Jane.

'Aunt Jane,' said Sally,
'remember how I **used to**
like spots? Well –'

'Remember?' asked Aunt Jane.
'How could I forget?
I already have your present
wrapped in lovely
spotty paper.'

'Oh,' said Sally again.

And Sally was very, very sad.

Nobody would listen to her.

She would be

stuck with spots

for ever and ever.

Sally went to visit Sam, her very best friend.

Sam didn't like spots.
He said that spots
made him dizzy.
Sam didn't have spots
on anything.

'I'm going to have to
live with spots
for ever and ever and ever,'
said Sally.
And she sobbed and sobbed.

Sam was shocked.
'We will have to think
of a plan,' he said.

So Sally stopped sobbing
and she and Sam
thought and thought
for a long time.

At last, Sam had an idea.

He whispered in Sally's ear.

Sally smiled.

'Thank you, Sam,' she said
and she gave him
a big kiss.
Two big pink spots
appeared on Sam's cheeks.

Then Sally and Sam
ran to Sally's house.

Sally whispered
in her Mum's ear.

At first Mum was shocked.
'What?' she said.
'No spots anymore?'

'No,' said Sally. '**No spots**.'

Mum said that she would help.

The next day was Saturday
and people were out
in their gardens
enjoying the sunshine.
They heard a loud noise
in the sky.

Please –

They looked up and
got a great surprise.
A plane flew overhead.
It was towing a big banner.
The banner had
big coloured letters
that everyone could see.

Grandma was shocked.
When she stopped being
shocked she said,
'I didn't know,'
and she stared up at the sky.

Grandad was shocked.
When he stopped being
shocked he said,
'I would never have guessed,'
and he rubbed his chin.

Please – no more

Aunt Jane was shocked.
When she stopped being
shocked she said,
'I never thought,'
and she shook her head.

Sally's Mum flew the plane
round and round
so that everyone could see
the big banner.

And that was the end of
Sally's spots.

When Sally was five she got
a dress with **swirls**
from Grandma,
some **stripy socks**
from Grandad,
a book with **zigzags**
from Aunt Jane,
a purse with **stars** on it
from her Mum and Dad.

And Sally got rid of
all her spots:
her spotty room,
her spotty clothes,
her spotty toys,
her spotty books.
She even got rid of
her spotty underwear.

Soon she had nothing left
with spots.

Except, of course . . .